This book belongs to

_____

For Mrs. Crawford,
with love and thanks for
all your encouragement

Henry Holt and Company, LLC
Publishers since 1866
175 Fifth Avenue
New York, New York 10010
www.HenryHoltKids.com

Henry Holt® is a registered trademark of Henry Holt and Company, LLC.
Copyright © 2008 by Sam Lloyd
First published in the United States in 2009 by Henry Holt and Company, LLC
Originally published in Great Britain in 2008 by Orchard Books
All rights reserved.
Distributed in Canada by H. B. Fenn and Company Ltd.

Library of Congress Cataloging-in-Publication Data
Lloyd, Sam. Chief Rhino to the rescue! / Sam Lloyd. —1st American ed.
p.   cm.
Summary: Although he sometimes mistakes lighted candles on a birthday cake for a house fire, the residents of
Whoops-a-Daisy World can always count on their strong and brave Fire Chief Rhino whenever a blaze threatens.
ISBN 978-0-8050-8821-2
[1. Fire fighters—Fiction. 2. Courage—Fiction. 3. Rhinoceroses—Fiction. 4. Animals—Fiction.] I. Title.
PZ7.L77875Ch 2009   [E]—dc22   2008036815

First American Edition—2009
Printed in March 2009 in Singapore by Tien Wah Press on acid-free paper. ∞

1 3 5 7 9 10 8 6 4 2

Chief Rhino
TO THE RESCUE

Sam Lloyd

Henry Holt and Company
New York

Meet Fire Chief Rhino. He's one of the bravest animals in Whoops-a-Daisy World. Whenever there's a fire, you can always count on him to save the day.

Chief Rhino likes to stay in peak physical
condition. You have to be strong to fight fires,
although there hasn't been a big fire in
Whoops-a-Daisy World for a long time…

...but suddenly Chief Rhino spots something!

"What the blazes?!" Chief Rhino exclaims.
"It looks like there's a fire at Number One
House Row! It's time for me to save the day!"

Chief Rhino dashes into the recreation room.
"Attention, team! Stop what you're doing.
We're needed, so let's go!"

Everybody gets dressed,

Kiss-it-Better Hospital

←Hospital

School

Shop Row

Blazes Fire station

Wee-ooo, wee-ooo!

Adam's Apples

And **AWAY** they go!
Wee-ooo, wee-ooo roars the
siren as they dash through
Whoops-a-Daisy World.

"This fire is a whopper,"
Chief Rhino announces.
"I need you all to be brave."

"Great balls of fire!" exclaims Chief Rhino. "This is even more serious than I thought. I'll need the ladder, the hose, and the breathing apparatus. Moose, when I shout 'NOW!' turn on the water."

"Yes, Chief!" answers Moose.

"Stand back!" instructs Chief Rhino. "I'm going in."

"Three...two...one...
NOW, Moose! NOW!"

Whoosh! The water will put out the fire.

Uh-oh... it was only the candles on Great-Granny Wrinkle's hundredth birthday cake!

"Flaming flumps of fire!" gasps Chief Rhino.
"How could I have made such a silly mistake?
Instead of saving the day, I've ruined it!"

"Now, don't you fret," says Great-Granny Wrinkle with a smile. "We all make mistakes. What's important is that you were trying to help."

"But I've ruined your cake," Chief Rhino says, sighing.

"Not at all!" Great-Granny Wrinkle giggles. "Elephants of my age don't have many teeth left, so mushy cake is perfect!"

Chief Rhino feels better.
"Let's give Great-Granny Wrinkle the most
super-sizzling party ever!" he says.

And they did...

...even with the soggy cake!